USBORNE HOTSHOTS
THE
EGYPTIANS

USBORNE HOTSHOTS

THE
EGYPTIANS

Edited by Rebecca Treays and Jane Chisholm

*Designed by Helen Westwood and
Heather Blackham*

*Illustrated by Richard Draper, Ian Jackson,
Joe McEwan, Sue Stitt and Gerald Wood*

*Series editor: Judy Tatchell
Series designer: Ruth Russell*

CONTENTS

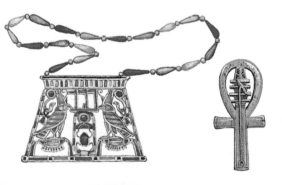

Who were the Egyptians?

This book is about the people who lived in Egypt more than 5,000 years ago. They founded one of the oldest civilizations in the world. At its peak, Ancient Egypt was a powerful trading nation, with a large empire. The Egyptians produced great works of art, including paintings, sculptures, temples and pyramids.

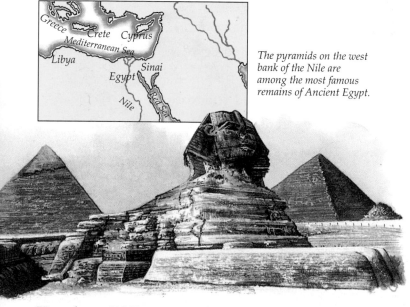

The pyramids on the west bank of the Nile are among the most famous remains of Ancient Egypt.

How long did Egyptian civilization last?

The Ancient Egyptian civilization lasted over 3,000 years. In 30BC, the Romans invaded and Egypt became part of the Roman empire.

The gold coffin of King Tutankhamun was decorated with precious jewels.

Experts divide Egyptian history into three main periods:

the **Old Kingdom** (2686-2181BC), when the pyramids were built;

the **Middle Kingdom** (2040-1786BC);

the **New Kingdom** (1567-1085BC). This is the period we know most about.

How do we know about Ancient Egypt?

We have plenty of information about how the Ancient Egyptians lived. The hot, dry climate helped to preserve many of the things they made. The pictures on this page show some of the things that archeologists have found in Egyptian tombs.

Wall painting

Egyptian picture writing

Much of what we know comes from the tombs of kings, queens and nobles. The insides were richly decorated with wall paintings, showing scenes from the person's life and the lives of the gods. People were often buried with their possessions.

Model animal

Furniture, chariots, glass, jewels and even fragments of clothes and food have all been found in tombs.

Dates

Most of the dates in this book have the letters BC after them. This stands for "Before Christ". BC dates are counted back from the birth of Christ. This means 3000BC is before 2000BC.

Many events can only be dated roughly. These dates have "c" before them, which stands for *circa*, the Latin for "about".

Bee hives made of pottery

Earrings

Preserved or mummified cat

5

Life in the country

Nearly all Egyptians lived as farmers in villages along the banks of the Nile, as this was the only place where they could grow crops. Very few people lived anywhere else because the rest of Egypt was just a huge, hot desert.

Every April, snow on the mountains in Ethiopia, south of Egypt, began to melt and flow into the Nile. In the following months, the river flooded the land in Egypt. The mud it left behind made rich, fertile soil.

The fertility of the land meant that the Egyptians had a varied diet. As well as the main crops of wheat and barley, they also grew melons, pomegranates, grapes, dates, figs, beans, peas, onions, garlic, leeks, lettuces and cucumbers.

Villages were built on high ground to avoid the floods.

Fields on higher ground were less productive, as the floods did not reach them every year.

Gauges were built on the riverbanks. Officials used them to check the water levels and plan for the year ahead.

The land was divided into small rectangular plots by a series of ditches and irrigation canals. The canals were used to store the flood water and supply it to the fields when needed. Each canal and ditch could be opened and closed.

The fields nearest the Nile were the most fertile.

Farmers marked the limits of their fields with boundary stones. It was a serious crime to move the stones or to block someone else's water supply.

The farming year

The flood season
(mid-July to mid-November)

In July, when the fields were covered with flood water, work came to a halt. Some farmers could just relax for a while, but others had to work on other projects for the king, such as building pyramids.

The growing season (mid-November to mid-March)

As the flood subsided, the farmers worked on the land. They scattered seeds by hand and drove animals across the fields to tread in the seed. In the following weeks, the farmers weeded and watered the crops.

The harvest (March to April)

Crops were gathered in March and April. Before they were harvested, taxmen came to assess how much grain each field would yield. From that they calculated how much each farmer should give to the king in taxes.

Summer
(mid-March to mid-July)

After the harvest, before the heat of the sun dried the soil out and made it too hard to dig, irrigation channels had to be repaired and new ones made, ready for the next flood.

Who ruled Eygpt?

Egypt was ruled by a king, called pharaoh, which means "great house". The Egyptians believed that the position of king had been introduced by the gods when the world was created. Egyptian kings were thought to be descended from the sun god, Re, who they believed was the very first king of Egypt.

A pharaoh and his queen

Until 3118BC, there were two Egyptian kings, one in Lower Egypt and one in Upper Egypt. In 3118BC, the country was united. The king's crown combined the crowns of Upper and Lower Egypt.

Red crown of   White crown of   Double
Upper Egypt   Lower Egypt   crown

The king's role

The king had absolute power. He also had a number of duties. It was his responsibility to rule justly and to maintain what the Egyptians called *ma'at*: the order, harmony and balance of the Universe. These are just some of the things he had to do.

Make decisions about government, law, trade and foreign policy.

Lead his army into battles.

Oversee the harvest and check the irrigation systems. People believed he could influence the weather and keep animals and plants fertile.

The king had to communicate with the gods. This statue shows the king with the god Horus, shown here as a falcon.

The queen

A king could have many wives but only one queen. She was not only the pharaoh's wife but also the eldest daughter of the last king and queen. This meant that the king had to marry his sister or half-sister.

Bronze statue of Queen Karomama, from the New Kingdom era.

How government was organized

Although the king was in charge of everything, he delegated the day to day management of affairs to officials. The most important officials were the two Viziers. One was in charge of Upper Egypt, and the other, Lower Egypt. Below them were governors who controlled rural districts, and mayors who controlled towns.

Scribes (see page 21) kept official records.

Taxation

The Egyptian government imposed a number of different taxes on the people. As there was no money, taxes were paid "in kind", with produce or work. The Viziers, with the help of their staff, controlled the taxation system.

Craftsmen had to give some of the goods they made.

Traders paid duty on imports and exports.

Hunters and fishermen paid taxes on what they killed.

One person in every household had to pay a work tax by doing public work for a few weeks every year.

There was a tax on land paid in grain and other produce.

Tribute was a tax paid by the people that the Egyptians conquered. This tribute bearer is from Syria.

Who did they worship?

The Egyptians had many gods and goddesses (see pages 12-13) who they believed could answer prayers and work miracles. Religious ceremonies played an important part in daily life.

Amulets

People kept charms called amulets to cast spells and to protect themselves from illness, accidents and any kind of danger or evil. You can sometimes see amulets on Egyptian jewels and furniture. If a prayer was answered or an illness cured, people usually left a gift at the temple to thank the god. Here are some of the most common amulets.

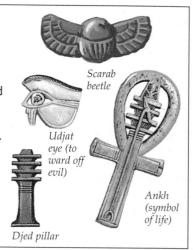

Scarab beetle

Udjat eye (to ward off evil)

Djed pillar

Ankh (symbol of life)

This is the festival of Bast, the cat goddess. Her statue is being led in a procession from her temple into the town.

The tall pointed towers are called obelisks. They are monuments to the sun god.

These cows will be sacrificed to Bast.

The statue of Bast is inside this golden shrine.

Temples

For the Egyptians, a temple was the home on Earth of the god or goddess it was dedicated to. It housed a statue, called a cult statue, through which the spirit of the god or goddess was believed to communicate.

A temple was not like a church, mosque or synagogue, where people gather together to worship. It was a private place. Only certain priests, priestesses, kings and queens were allowed inside, except on very rare occasions.

Most temples had an open courtyard, a pillared hall called the hypostyle, and a sanctuary. The sanctuary contained the Holy of Holies, a shrine where the cult statue was kept. Ordinary people were never allowed beyond the courtyard.

Each day at sunrise, noon and sunset, the priests and priestesses made offerings to the god. This was a way of saying thank you for all the god had done.

A typical New Kingdom temple

The temple walls are decorated with paintings and carvings.

Gods and goddesses

There were dozens of Egyptian gods and goddesses. The most important gods, such as Amun, had a home town where their main temple was situated. They also had shrines across the country. Other gods had only a local following. A few had altars only in people's homes.

Most gods and goddesses were represented as forces of nature such as water or air. They might also be associated with certain jobs such as weaving or farming, or identified with a certain animal. Here are some important Egyptian gods and goddesses.

Horus, son of Osiris and Isis, inherited the throne of Egypt. Animal: falcon.

Isis, goddess of crafts, wife and sister of Osiris.

Amun, King of the gods in the New Kingdom. Animals: goose and ram.

Bast, the cat goddess, who represented the healing power of the sun.

Anubis, god of the dead and embalming*. Animal: jackal.

Re, the sun god and creator.

*See page 14.

Tawaret, *a hippopotamus who looked after pregnant women and babies.*

Bes *the dwarf, jester of the gods, protected people's homes and children.*

Thoth, *god of wisdom. Animals: baboon and ibis.*

Hathor, *wife of Horus, goddess of love, beauty and joy. Animal: cow.*

Sobek, *god of water. Animal: crocodile.*

Set, *god of deserts, storms and trouble. Animals: ass, pig and hippopotamus.*

Osiris, *King of Egypt, who became ruler of the Dead. He introduced vines and grain.*

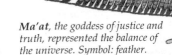

Ma'at, *the goddess of justice and truth, represented the balance of the universe. Symbol: feather.*

Mummies and the afterlife

The Egyptians believed that after people died their spirits went to a place called the Next World. For this to happen, they thought that the body itself must survive. They developed an elaborate way of preserving bodies, called embalming, to stop them from decaying. But this was very expensive, so only kings, nobles and the very wealthy could afford it.

The embalming process

When a man died, priests said prayers over him. His body was then washed and taken to the *wabet*, the embalmers' workshop.

First, a cut was made in his left side. The internal organs were removed and stored in containers called canopic jars. Then the body was covered with natron (a salt) to dry it out. After a few days, the insides were stuffed with linen or sawdust. The body was wrapped in linen with jewels and amulets between the layers.

The wrapped body, which we call a mummy, was placed in a coffin.

Canopic jars

The embalmer wore a jackal mask to represent Anubis, the god of embalmers (see page 12).

Many coffins were decorated with gold and inlaid with semi-precious stones. Some consisted of a nest of two or three coffins, one inside the other.

The funeral

A funeral procession

The body was led in a procession to a tomb. Final prayers were said. The coffin was put inside a sarcophagus (stone coffin), with things to help the person in the Next World. These included a special book called *The Book of the Dead*. The priests then left, sweeping away their footprints as they went.

The Next World

The Egyptians believed that the spirit of the dead person crossed the River of Death into the Next World. With the help of amulets and a *Book of the Dead*, which contained maps and spells, he had

to pass through the Twelve Gates, guarded by snakes. Then he met the 42 Assessors, a group of judges.

He had to swear he had not committed certain crimes. Then he went to the Judgment Hall, where his heart was weighed against the Feather of Truth. If they weighed the same, he went to a happy land, where he was met by his dead relations. If not, he went to a hellish place full of monsters.

The pyramids

Egyptian kings had massive tombs built for themselves. The Old Kingdom kings developed the famous and enormous pyramid-shaped tombs, many of which still stand today on the west bank of the Nile. The earliest ones were called step pyramids, as they were built in steps. The Egyptians may have believed that the dead king climbed up the pyramid to the stars.

The first step pyramid was built for King Zoser, and was designed by his architect Imhotep.

The pyramid was surrounded by a vast enclosure, 547 x 278m (1,790 x 912ft).

Inside the enclosure were buildings finely decorated on the outside. Most of them were just filled with rubble.

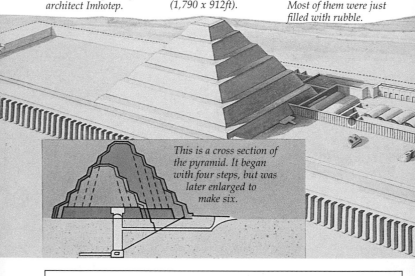

This is a cross section of the pyramid. It began with four steps, but was later enlarged to make six.

Building a pyramid

The pyramids were built in layers. Huge blocks of stone were dragged up large earth ramps. The ramp was raised, widened and lengthened, layer by layer, as the pyramid got taller. It took thousands of men up to twenty years to build a pyramid.

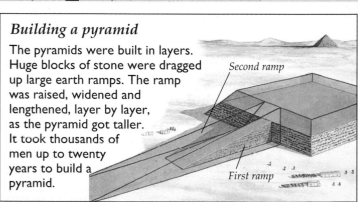

Second ramp

First ramp

Smooth-sided pyramids

Later pyramids had smooth sides. This may have been to represent the rays of the sun, up which the king could climb to the sun god, Re.

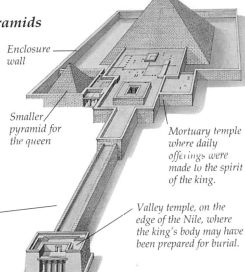

Enclosure wall

Smaller pyramid for the queen

Mortuary temple where daily offerings were made to the spirit of the king.

This reconstruction is based on the pyramid of King Sahure at Abusir.

A covered causeway linked the valley and the mortuary temples.

Valley temple, on the edge of the Nile, where the king's body may have been prepared for burial.

The sphinx

Workmen building King Khufu's pyramid at Gizah were left with an enormous outcrop of rock. They carved it into a sphinx, a creature with a lion's body and the king's head. The sphinx was supposed to guard the pyramid.

The lion's body represents the sun god, Re.

The Valley of the Kings

The pyramids were frequently robbed, so New Kingdom kings chose instead to be buried in tombs cut deep into the sides of cliffs. These are found in the Valley of the Kings on the west bank of the Nile. The tombs don't look very grand from the outside, but they were lavishly decorated inside.

The Egyptian army

During the Old and Middle Kingdoms, the Egyptian army consisted of the king's bodyguard and a small army of professional soldiers. Ordinary men could be called up in emergencies, but most had no military training, so weren't much use.

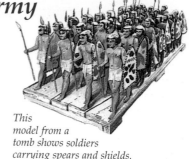

This model from a tomb shows soldiers carrying spears and shields.

By the New Kingdom, the need to drive out invaders and the desire to conquer an empire meant that the army needed to be reorganized. Horses and chariots were introduced, volunteers were recruited and trained, and the army increased in size.

The army was split into divisions, each made up of 4,000 foot soldiers and 1,000 charioteers. Each division was named after a god. Divisions were further divided into 20 companies of 200 foot soldiers each.

Standard (flag) bearer

Foot soldier

Charioteer

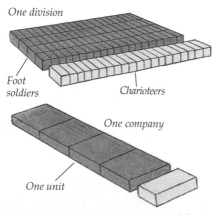

One division

Foot soldiers

Charioteers

One company

One unit

Companies were then split into four units of 50 men, who normally shared barracks in groups of ten. 25 two-man chariots were attached to each company. The charioteers were the elite troops, because of the cost of the equipment and the skill and training involved. In battle, they always fought in front.

Weapons and training

Egyptian soldiers had to be able to fight with a variety of weapons, including battle axes, maces, spears, swords, daggers and bows and arrows. However, each unit tended to specialize in the use of one particular weapon. Young soldiers were given a tough training, which included long route marches.

Spear

Scimitar

Weapons were made of bronze or wood.

Dagger

Javelin

Axes

Bow and arrows

Mace

Empire building

The armies of the New Kingdom set about building an empire. The king often led foreign campaigns himself. At its height, the Egyptian empire stretched from Syria to the Fourth Cataract of the Nile. (A cataract is a place where large rocks block the path of a river. They formed important boundaries in ancient times.) The Egyptians became very rich by trading with their empire and claiming tribute (see page 9) from their subjects.

Under Egyptian control

Area of Egyptian influence

On campaign, the army would set up camps like this one.

Tents were laid out in rows. The king's was in the middle.

A defensive mound with shields on top protected the camp.

Sentries

Messengers leaving the camp

Reading and writing

The Egyptians were one of the earliest people to invent a form of writing. Their "alphabet" was not made up of letters, like the one we use today, but of pictures and signs. We call Egyptian writing hieroglyphs, which means "holy writing". This is because the Egyptians thought their knowledge of writing had been given to them by Thoth, the god of wisdom.

How hieroglyphs work

Egyptian writing consisted of over 700 signs, most of which are recognizable as pictures of things. Each sign could either stand for a specific object or a certain sound, as shown on the right.

Hieroglyphs can be written from left to right, right to left, or down. If the animals or people are facing left, you read from left to right. If they are facing right, you read from right to left.

Mouth – "r"   Loaf – "t"

Flax – "h"

Owl – "m"   Face – "hr"

Goose – "sa"

Bolt – "s"   Water – "n"

Some hieroglyphs

These hieroglyphs are read from left to right.

These are the same hieroglyphs, but read from right to left.

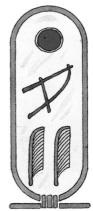

Pharaoh's names were always written inside an oval shape called a cartouche. This is a cartouche of the pharaoh Meyre.

Scribes

Egyptian hieroglyphs were extremely complicated. It took years of study to learn them all properly. People called scribes were specially trained to read and write. Their skill brought them power and status. Scribes could get good jobs in temples or in government. They often didn't have to pay taxes.

What did they write with?

The scribes wrote with ink and brushes on a special sort of paper called papyrus, which was made from reeds. They also wrote things on pieces of broken pottery known as ostraca.

Papyrus scroll

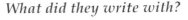

Palette of inks *Brushes*

Shorthand

Later, the Egyptians developed two shorthand scripts which were easier versions of hieroglyphs. Hieroglyphs were kept for inscriptions on temples and public buildings.

This shorthand script, known as hieratic, was in use during the Old Kingdom.

This script, known as demotic, was developed later.

Schools, medicine and science

Egyptian schools were only for the boys of wealthy families. Most children didn't go to school. Instead, boys were taught a trade by their fathers, while girls helped their mothers at home.

A temple school

Most Egyptian schools were attached to temples. Boys went to school when they were about seven years old. They learned to read and write, and spent most of their time copying texts.

The teacher is a scribe.

The boys are writing on broken pieces of pottery. Papyrus is too expensive.

Papyrus with mathematical calculations

At nine or ten, a boy could go on to another school. Here he learned how to write letters and legal documents. He could also study a range of subjects including history, literature, geography, religion, languages, account-keeping, mathematics and medicine.

Medical school

There were probably special medical schools in Egypt, because Egyptian doctors were famous for their skill. Some used to travel to other countries to treat foreign royalty.

Religion also played an important part in medicine. People often went to the temples to ask a god for a cure.

Egyptian doctors understood a fair amount about how the body worked. They knew about the nervous system and a little about the brain. They also knew that the heart acted like a pump.

22

Measuring

Measurements were based on the body of an adult. Elbow to fingertip was called one cubit. A cubit was divided into seven hands, each four fingers wide.

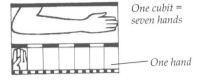

One cubit = seven hands

One hand

A water clock

Water clocks

Like us, the Egyptians divided each day into 24 hours. They told the time using water clocks. These were pots with hours marked off on the inside. They were filled with water and a small spout was opened at the bottom. As the water dripped out, the number of marks that were exposed indicated the time.

Calendars

The Egyptians were interested in the stars and planets. They used their knowledge to work out several calendars. One calendar was based on a star called Sopdet. The Egyptians noticed that Sopdet disappeared below the horizon at the same time each year, and reappeared just before sunrise 70 days later.

This happened just when the Nile began to rise for the annual floods. It became the date of their New Year. Another calendar was based on the cycle of the moon. When the Romans conquered Egypt they were so impressed that they adopted it themselves. It was used throughout Europe until the 16th century.

This Ancient Egyptian drawing shows the stars represented as gods.

Getting around

As most people in Ancient Egypt lived close to the Nile, boats were the best way to travel.

The Nile flows from south to north, but the wind usually blows from the north. This means that boats can drift downstream on the current, but if they raise their sails, the wind will carry them back upstream.

The Egyptian hieroglyph for "south" or "upstream" shows a boat with its sail up. The hieroglyph for "north" or "downstream" shows a boat with its sail down.

Here are some different kinds of Ancient Egyptian boats.

Old Kingdom fishing boat

Early reed boat

Old Kingdom cargo boat

New Kingdom trading ship

Barges were used to transport heavy cargo.

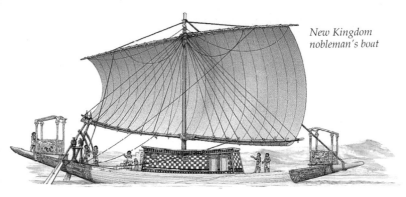

New Kingdom nobleman's boat

Funeral boat used to transport bodies of the wealthy to their tombs.

How far did they sail?

Egyptian traders sailed to ports in the Eastern Mediterranean and the Red Sea. Some even went all the way to Punt, a land somewhere in East Africa. They went looking for valuable myrrh trees which they used to make incense.

An expedition leaves Punt to return to Egypt.

Travel by land

If they couldn't get somewhere by boat, most people had to walk. The very rich were carried on special chairs. Merchants used donkeys to carry goods.

Crafts and trades

Most Egyptians were farmers, but there were also other jobs, crafts and trades that people could do. The most highly skilled craftsmen and women worked in temple and palace workshops, or on the estates of nobles. Village craftsmen made goods for the local market.

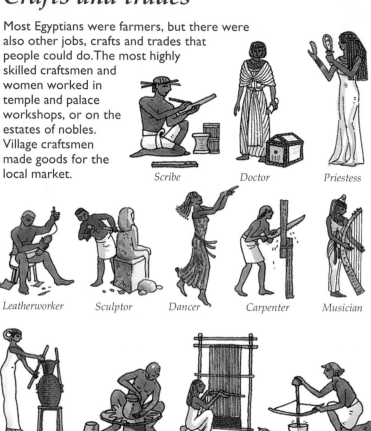

Scribe

Doctor

Priestess

Leatherworker

Sculptor

Dancer

Carpenter

Musician

Perfume maker

Potter

Weaver

Stone vase maker

Tools and techniques

Experts have been able to learn a lot about the techniques of Egyptian craftsmen from paintings and models left in tombs, as well as from the objects they made. On the opposite page is a selection of different Egyptian crafts, showing some of the tools and techniques that were used.

This painting shows goldsmiths at work.

Weaving

The first looms were laid out on the ground and held in place with pegs.

Later looms were upright. These were more practical because they took up less space.

Many weavers were women.

Carpentry

Copper and bronze carpentry tools with wooden handles

Using a saw to cut wood

Making a hollow with a mallet and chisel

Polishing wood with sandstone

Leather working

Leather was used to make bags, sandals, shields, arrow quivers (holders) and furniture.

Pottery

Pots were shaped on a wheel turned by hand by the potter's assistant.

The pots were baked in a wood-burning kiln.

Metalworking

A technique called lost-wax casting was used to make fine statues and ornaments. This process is still in use.

1. A wax model of the statue was made around a small clay core. It was then covered in more clay, held in place with pegs.

2. The clay was heated, the wax melted and was poured away.

3. The empty space was filled with molten metal. When it cooled, the clay was broken, leaving a metal statue.

Fashion

Most Egyptians were too poor and too hot to worry much about what they looked like. But it was important for rich people to keep up appearances and to look good. Unlike today, however, fashions stayed the same for about a thousand years.

Children often had shaved heads with one long braid left at the back.

The basic costume for a woman was a linen dress held up by two straps.

Hair padded with ornaments

Some fancy kilts were pleated.

The basic costume for a man was a linen kilt, wrapped around and tied at the waist.

Older and more important men wore long kilts.

Some men shaved their heads and wore wigs.

This rich woman is wearing a dress with hundreds of glass beads sewn into it.

Patterned dress made of stripes of overlapping pieces of material

Men and women in the New Kingdom wore pleated tunics or dresses and flowing cloaks.

Shoes and gloves

Sandals and gloves were worn on special occasions. These were found in the tomb of the King Tutankhamun.

Jewels

Everyone in Egypt wore jewels. The rich wore pieces made from gold and silver and inlaid with semi-precious stones and glass. Poorer people wore copper or faience (a sort of glazed pottery).

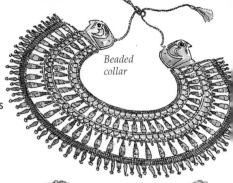

Beaded collar

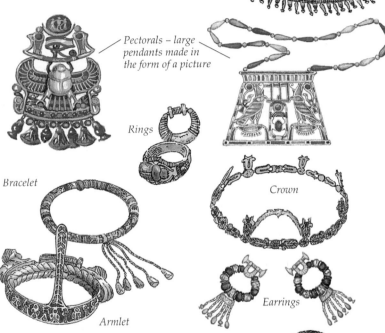

Pectorals – large pendants made in the form of a picture

Rings

Bracelet

Crown

Armlet

Earrings

Cosmetics

Both men and women painted their faces. Lip and eye paints were made from minerals which were ground into a powder. The powder was stored in jars and then mixed with oil or water.

Mirror made from highly polished silver

Eye paint also kept away the flies.

Entertainment

Paintings and objects left in tombs show us what the Egyptians did for entertainment. Plays were performed at temples which told tales about the gods. Religious festivals and processions also provided a fun day out.

The river

The Nile was an important source of sports and entertainment. Many Egyptians would take a day hunting, fishing, swimming and picnicking on its banks.

This man is having a refreshing dip.

Fishing with a harpoon

Hippopotamus hunting was very dangerous. It usually took a team of men, with harpoons, ropes and nets, to catch one.

Games and toys

The Egyptians had several types of board games using counters or pegs, like the two shown here. No rules have survived, so no one knows how to play them.

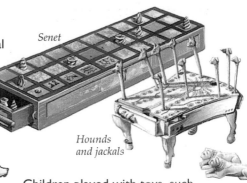

Senet

Hounds and jackals

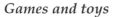

Toy dog

Balls

Hippo

Children played with toys, such as spinning tops, dolls and wooden animals on wheels. Some toys even had moving parts, like the dog on the left whose mouth opened.

Pets and zoos

The Egyptians were animal lovers and kept a variety of pets, including cats, dogs, monkeys and geese. Sometimes a dog's collar was buried with its owner. Some pharaohs seem to have collected exotic animals and even set up their own zoos.

Music and parties

Wealthy Egyptians often threw lavish parties. Groups of singers, dancers, musicians, jugglers and acrobats were hired to entertain the guests.

This wall-painting shows musicians playing a harp, lute, pipes and a lyre.

Egyptian dancers

Index

This book is based on material previously published in *Early Civilization* in the *Usborne Illustrated World History* series, *Ancient Egypt* in the *Usborne Pocket Guide* series, and *Who Built the Pyramids?* in the *Usborne Starting Point History* series.

First published in 1996 by Usborne Publishing Ltd, Usborne House, 83-85 Saffron Hill, London, EC1N 8RT, England. Copyright © 1996, 1995, 1991, 1981. Usborne Publishing Ltd.

First published in America August 1996. UE   Printed in Italy.